FOR ANDREW & PATRICE —S. G. R.

I AM DEEPLY GRATEFUL TO THE ESTATE OF ROY LICHTENSTEIN
FOR PERMITTING ME TO USE ROY'S ART FOR THIS BOOK. AT CHRONICLE BOOKS
MY THANKS GO TO MY DEDICATED EDITOR, VICTORIA ROCK; HER ASSISTANT, TAYLOR NORMAN;
AND OUR TALENTED DESIGNER, SARA GILLINGHAM. A SPECIAL THANK-YOU TO PETER HUESTIS
AT THE NATIONAL GALLERY OF ART. I AM GRATEFUL TO MY WRITER FRIENDS FOR THEIR
ENTHUSIASTIC CRITIQUES, AND TO MY AGENT AND DEAR FRIEND, GEORGE NICHOLSON,
AND HIS COLLEAGUE ERICA SILVERMAN. LASTLY, A BIG THANK YOU TO MY SON, ANDREW RUBIN,
WHO DELIGHTED IN THIS PROJECT FROM THE START AND HELPED ME BRING IT TO LIFE.

LIBRARY OF CONGRESS CATALOGING-IN-PUBLICATION DATA

RUBIN, SUSAN GOLDMAN, AUTHOR.
ROY'S HOUSE / BY SUSAN GOLDMAN RUBIN.
PAGES CM

ISBN 978-1-4521-1185-8 (ALK. PAPER)
1. LICHTENSTEIN, ROY, 1923-1997—JUVENILE LITERATURE. I. TITLE.

ND237.L627R83 2016
759.13—DC23

MANUFACTURED IN CHINA.

DESIGN BY SARA GILLINGHAM STUDIO.
TYPESET IN P22 POP ART AND ROY LICHTENSTEIN.

10 9 8 7 6 5 4 3 2 1

CHRONICLE BOOKS LLC
680 SECOND STREET
SAN FRANCISCO, CALIFORNIA 94107

CHRONICLE BOOKS—WE SEE THINGS DIFFERENTLY.
BECOME PART OF OUR COMMUNITY AT WWW.CHRONICLEKIDS.COM.

ROY'S HOUSE

COME ON IN!

BY SUSAN GOLDMAN RUBIN  chronicle books·san francisco   ART BY ROY LICHTENSTEIN

IN ROY'S HOUSE,
A TELEPHONE RINGS.

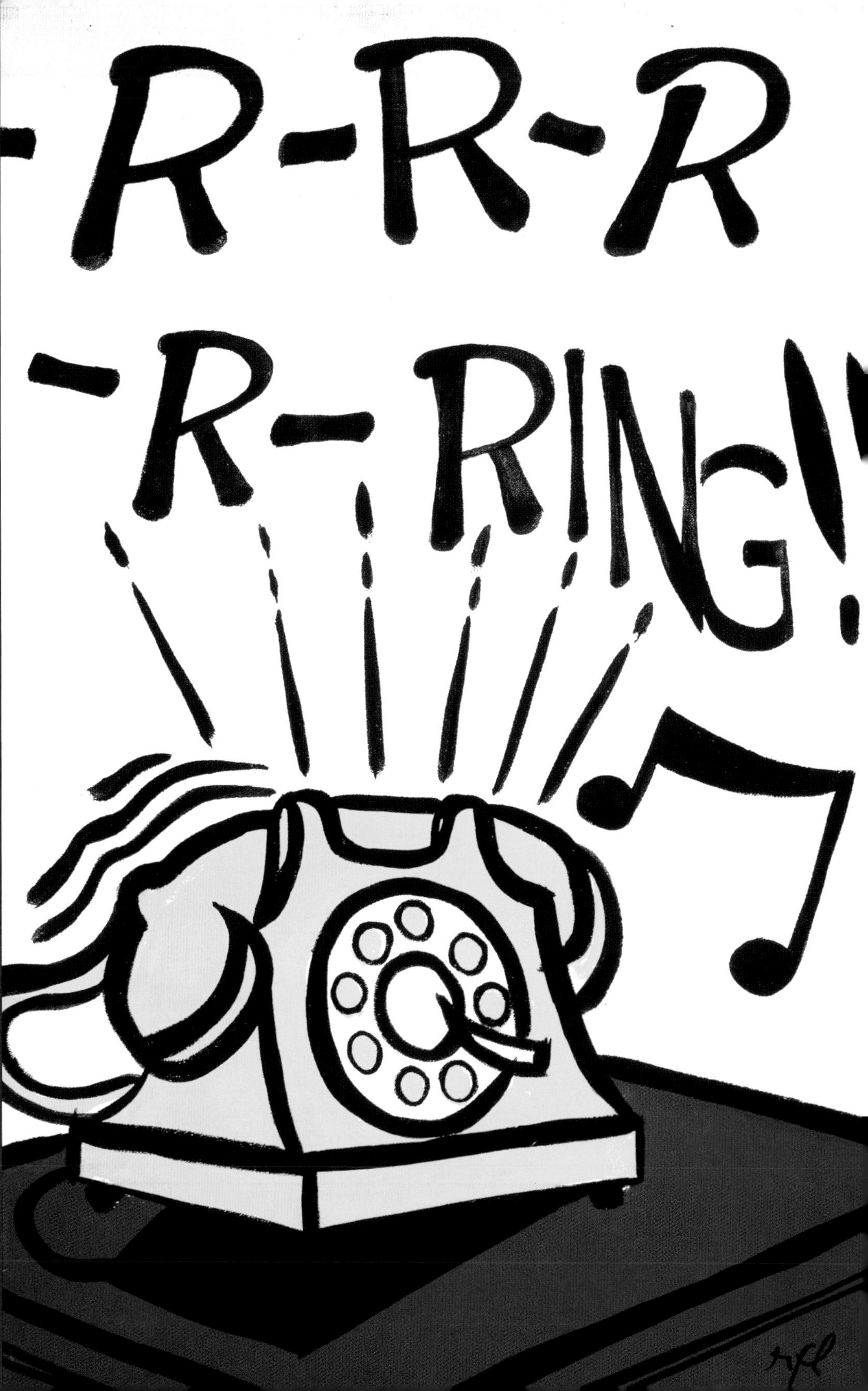
-R-R-R
-R-R-RING!!

ROY'S LIVING ROOM HAS A GREAT BIG COUCH. THERE IS ROOM FOR MANY FRIENDS.

THERE IS A SMALL YELLOW
CHAIR FOR READING. AND A
LAMP THAT IS SHINING BRIGHT.

SOMETHING SMELLS GOOD
IN THE KITCHEN.

ROY IS
BAKING A PIE.

WE CAN SIT UP AT THE COUNTER
AND HAVE A TASTY SNACK . . .

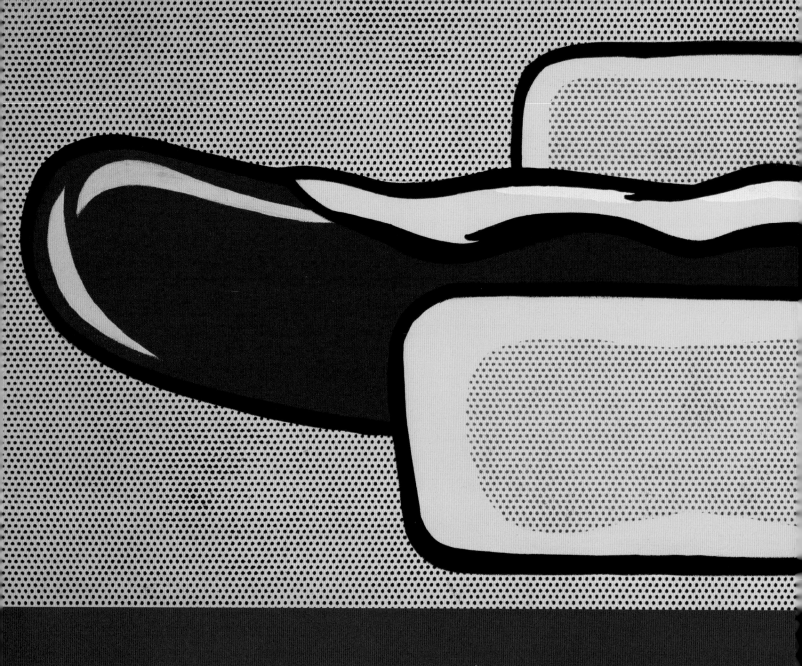

MAYBE A HOT

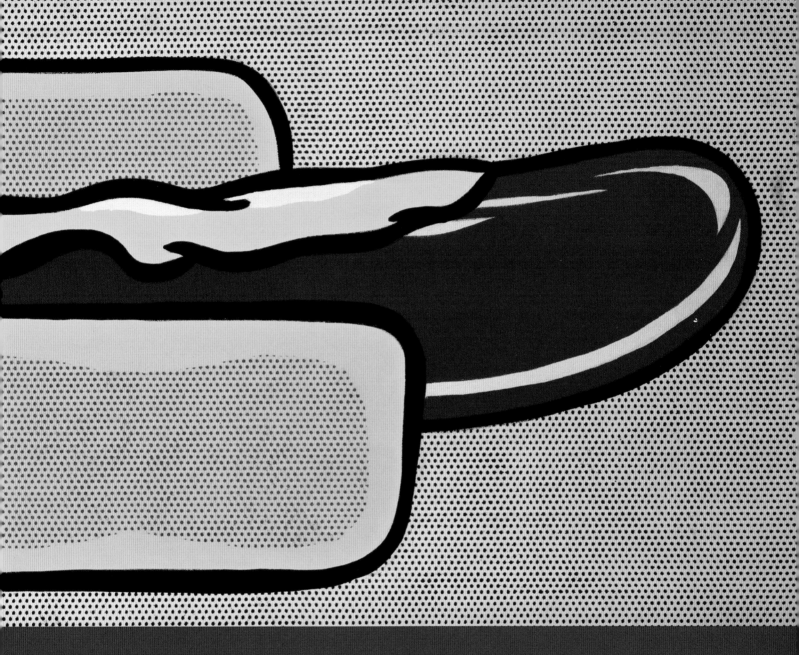

DOG IN A BUN,

A DRINK WITH A STRAW,

THEN YUMMY CHERRY PIE.

THE BATHROOM HAS A TUB
AND SINK. WE CAN WASH
OUR STICKY HANDS.

IN ROY'S HOUSE, THERE IS A BEDROOM WITH YELLOW PILLOWS AND LAMPS.

LET'S GO INTO THE STUDIO.

ROY PAINTS PICTURES HERE!

HE KEEPS HIS BRUSHES IN A JAR, READY TO PAINT

A BUNCH OF PRETTY FLOWERS,

OR THE SUNSET IN THE SKY.

WE CAN PAINT
PICTURES TOO.

IF WE MAKE A MESS,
WE WILL CLEAN UP.

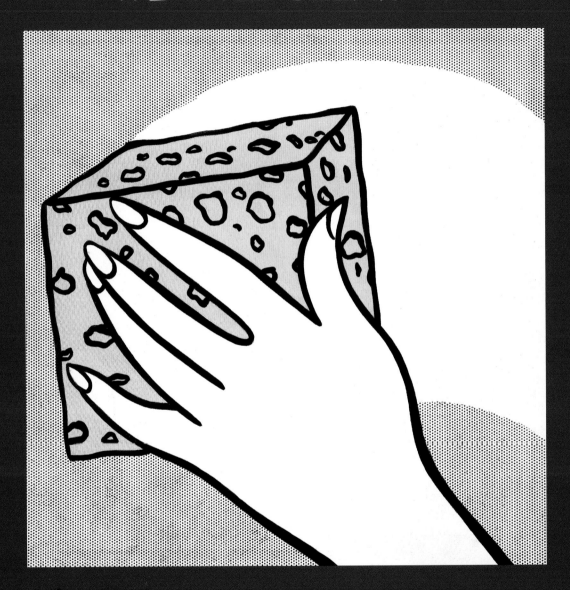

WIPE, WIPE WITH A SOAPY SPONGE.

GET READY. HERE COMES COMPANY.

Photograph © by Ken Heyman.

Photograph © by Laurie Lambrecht.

AUTHOR'S NOTE

ROY LICHTENSTEIN was born on October 27, 1923, in New York City. As a boy he loved to draw, and by the time he was fifteen he knew he wanted to be an artist. He studied art at Ohio State University and later taught there.

In 1961, he started painting big cartoon figures. He copied the newspaper process of printing shades of color with tiny dots. But Roy enlarged the dots and painted them by hand with bold black outlines and flat primary colors. His first show shocked critics in 1962. But by 1963 he was earning enough money from his art to give up teaching.

Roy and some other artists of the time turned to popular culture for inspiration. Critics dubbed them "Pop Artists." Roy's subject matter ranged from comic books and bubble gum wrappers to advertisements, signs, and reproductions of art by twentieth-century masters. Museums and collectors throughout the world bought and exhibited his work, and he received many awards. He continued painting until he died on September 19, 1997, at the age of 73. His work is still enjoyed today, and Roy is recognized as a major American artist.

You can see *House I*, which is featured on the title page of this book, at the National Gallery of Art in Washington, D.C. The sculpture was created after Roy died, based on his specifications.

MORE ABOUT THE WORKS OF ROY LICHTENSTEIN FEATURED IN THIS BOOK (IN ORDER OF APPEARANCE)

House I, 1996/1998. Painted aluminum, 115 x 176 x 52 inches (292.1 x 447 x 132.1 cm).

Hot Dog with Mustard, 1963. Magna on canvas, 18 x 48 inches (45.7 x 121.9 cm).

Collage for Flowers in Glass, 1990. Tape, painted and printed paper on board, 40¼ x 30⅛ inches (102.2 x 76.5 cm).

-R-R-R-R-Ring!!, 1962. Oil on canvas, 24 x 16 inches (60.9 x 40.6 cm).

Sandwich and Soda, 1964. Screenprint on clear plastic, 20 x 24 inches (50.8 x 60.9 cm).

Sinking Sun, 1964. Oil and Magna on canvas, 68 x 80 inches (172.7 x 203.2 cm).

Interior with African Mask, 1991. Oil and Magna on canvas, 114 x 146 inches (289.5 x 370.8 cm).

Cherry Pie, 1962. Oil on canvas, 20 x 24 inches (50.8 x 60.9 cm).

Brushstroke, 1965. Screenprint on heavy, white wove paper, 23 x 29 inches (58.4 x 73.6 cm).

Interior with Yellow Chair, 1993. Oil and Magna on canvas, 80 x 80 inches (203.2 x 203.2 cm).

Bathroom, 1961. Oil on canvas, 45 x 69 inches (114.3 x 175.2 cm).

Sponge II, 1962. Oil on canvas, 36 x 36 inches (91.4 x 91.4 cm).

Still Life with Goldfish (and Painting of Golf Ball), 1972. Oil and Magna on canvas, 52 x 42 inches (132 x 106 cm).

Interior with Mobile, 1992. Oil and Magna on canvas, 130 x 171 inches (330.2 x 434.3 cm).

Knock Knock, 1961. Ink on paper, 20¼ x 19¾ inches (51.4 x 50.1 cm).

Kitchen Stove, 1961. Oil on canvas, 68 x 68 inches (172.7 x 172.7 cm).

Artist's Studio, 1973. Oil and Magna on canvas, 60 x 74 inches (152.4 x 187.9 cm).

Collage for Interior with Painting of House, 1997. Tape, painted and printed paper on board, 30½ x 30 inches (77.4 x 76.2 cm).

Interior with Built-In Bar, 1991. Oil and Magna on canvas, 114 x 164 inches (289.5 x 416.5 cm).

Still Life in Yellow and Black, 1972. Oil and Magna on canvas, 56 x 40 inches (137.1 x 101.6 cm).